FEEDING HOLY CATS

Feeding Holy Cats

Ain't Got No Press

Front Cover Photo, Design, and Layout ~ Rick Lupert
Back Cover and Authors Photo ~ Marcella Marlowe

The author lives in fear of forgetting to thank people who deserve heart-felt thanks and would therefore like to thank everyone alive today on planet Earth and everyone who has ever lived on planet Earth for everything that they've ever done which has ultimately led to the existence of an ecosphere in which this book could be produced.

Thanks also to Amélie Frank and Cassowary Press for publishing the first edition of this book.

(818) 904-1021

or

15522 Stagg Street
Van Nuys, CA 91406

or

Rick@PoetrySuperHighway.com

or

http://PoetrySuperHighway.com/

First CreateSpace ~ July, 2008

ISBN: 978-0-9727555-7-3 $8.00

TABLE OF CONTENTS

* Asterisk

INTRODUCTION

Sunday December 26, 1999 I received a phone call from one of my co-workers asking if I could leave for Israel three days later because she was sick and couldn't go. A solid three seconds of thought later I had determined that there was absolutely no reason why I couldn't. So I did. And there I was for ten days leading a group of college students around the Holy Land with my guitar at hand and cats everywhere.

This book isn't really about the cats, but trust me, they were there; at the Western Wall, on top of Masada, in front of the desert hotel at four in the morning, and outside of Mr. Li's Kosher Chinese Food restaurant in Jerusalem. What can one say? "Meow," I suppose.

Israel is an amazing country. At any location you are a stone's throw from several other countries. If you've ever watched the news, you know that sometimes stones are thrown.

Everything in Israel is at least four thousand years old. Even the buildings constructed last week are four thousand years old. It's just how it works there. Have you ever been in a four thousand year old building? Don't answer now. Just find one and go in. All the people are also four thousand years old. You can see it in the eyes of the men selling spices in Jerusalem's Jewish Market. You can see it in the eyes of the eighteen year old rifle toting soldiers standing next to flower stands before Shabbat. You can see it in the eyes of Israeli babies. Four thousand years old . . .

So there I was, amidst everything old, using *my* poet's eye to see, and my poet's pen to remember. It's all about remembering . . . I hope the glossary helps.

March 3, 2000

to women named Michal everywhere

First Observation

A sign on a road
in the Upper Galilee
says "Dangerous Curves"
I've known so many women like that

Hagoshrim

New Years on the Kibbutz
where they invented the Epilady
I have the smoothest legs of the millennium

Looking For Luau In All the Wrong Places

Between the Upper Galilee
and the Golan Heights
It's called the Hula Valley
Yet there is no Don Ho

Talking With Arabs

Walking through Arab village
Family invites us in for Orange Soda
mixed nuts and conversation
We only have twenty minutes
which is enough
to talk about football
North Carolina
and how they feel like second class citizens
They have beautiful couches
and children
more of both on the way
peace now
peace now

The Dark Side of Zionism

Driving night time road
from ancient Galilee to Tel Aviv
Israeli radio sings

> *I'm your Tamagotchi*
> *Happy that you love me*
> *We will be together*
> *Forever ever ever*

One can only feel so holy
in these situations

The Hula Valley

Riding across the Hula Valley
in jeeps and mountain bike
passed destroyed Syrian bunkers
fenced off mine fields

Imported Eucalyptus trees
which didn't quite drink the swamps
The canal which did

I imagine sitting in a bomb shelter
underneath the dining room or
working the fields in my tractor
with steel bullet shields
and an Uzi at my feet

What a beautiful valley
gazelles
birds
green green green
Grass begins to grow through the Syrian gun turrets
I can see it happening

Michal

Sabra wildflower
with blue eyes
and Princess Leia hair
sculpts a bird out of blue Play-dough
gives it to me
with tea
and promises of electronic letters to come
Schedules prevent good-bye hug
at end of two day fiesta
I leave letter on hotel stationary
with milk chocolate and local leaf
Hope for the best

One Hump or Two

We pass by the Camel Comedy Club
in the old city of Jaffa
Take my humps please

We Get Wet in Israel

Much needed rain
as we leave cosmopolitan Tel Aviv
for holier destinations

It's the stuff you need to make the desert bloom
We've been given umbrellas
We're good

Shikola maneuvers our bus like Caesar's barge
Marcella notices our window is leaking
She doesn't mind
Just wants us to know

Feeding Holy Cats

I've fed half the cats in the Negev Desert today
I'll get the rest tomorrow

It's the Salt

The Dead Sea evaporates more each year
which is good because
there's more room on the beach
and bad because
soon our canoes won't work

Sandstorm

The desert wind is blowing
It tries to blow me
I don't let it
I'm not that easy

Let's Get This Straight

All roads lead to Jerusalem
Except for the ones that don't
But I'm not talking about those roads

Leave Your Clothes in the Lobby

The coat-racks
in the lobby
of the hotel
can fit fourteen coats
or fourteen hats
or any combination
of coats and hats
Probably you could get away
with a higher number
if you toss scarves
into the mixture

Comment Overheard on a Jerusalem Hotel Couch

Come on you two, get a raincoat.

At the Kotel

Bushes emerge from the Western Wall
One wonders if Herod was a gardener

I daven on the men's side of the Wall
Egalitarianism hasn't reached the Old City

Paper yarmulke on my head
Right hand touching Roman stone

I say all the words I can remember
A boy becomes bar mitzvah behind me

We finish at the same time
Back away, the Wall gets bigger

The sun melts winter away
Lights up the wall

Once again
Jerusalem of Gold

Doing the Numbers at Yad Vashem

It takes six hundred and seventy three shelves
with five thousand seven hundred
        and eighty four books
to list the six million Jews
murdered in the Holocaust

Too Many Shoes

It doesn't hit you 'til you see the piles of shoes
in the room with the loud silence
You have to walk out
before you lose your hearing altogether

Waiting for a Taxi in Jerusalem

You can see your entire life
drive before your eyes

Shabbat at the Kotel

Ten thousand dancing Chasids
I'm exaggerating of course
But you wouldn't know it from the fervor
so thick
the Palestinians cut slabs of it
out of the air to make coats
and keep warm

On Ben Yehuda Street

You love love
says the girl

in the store
behind the counter

She can see it in my eyes
admits to also loving love

We'd head off together
if we lived on the same continent

Medical Advice From the Religious Lady

They should play harps
instead of using Prozac
says the woman at the Biblical Harp Store
I suppose at the Prozac store
they don't speak too highly of Biblical Harps either

The Cats in Jerusalem

don't seem to care for Chinese food

Mahane Yehuda, Friday Afternoon

Religious man
blows his horn
in the Jewish Market
letting people know
the Sabbath is on it's way
I drink warm Coca Cola
Take his cue
buying Sabbath flowers
under open air Friday

Oops

Ten shequels solves the problem
of the broken glass candle holder
in the Jerusalem boutique
I am warned about gravity
and instructed to never touch
anything again

Let's Sum it Up

In Israel
I fell in love
with at least six women
named Michal
It's that kind of country

Flying Home from Tel Aviv

I am in the airport
I am on the plane

I am in the air
I am drinking water

Water leaks from plane ceiling
Doesn't seem right

I have four shequels in my pocket
I am thirty one thousand feet and climbing

It is a different time everywhere
Girl next to me laughs like a Canadian
            living in the Dakotas

I am duty free
I am salute the other passengers

I am still climbing
I am eighteen hours away

I am gone from Holy Land
I am hands smell like banana

I am leave guitar on Tarmac
I am in flight movie

I am eat
I am sleep

I am fly, fly, fly

GLOSSARY

Arabs A swarthy race occupying Arabia, and numerous in Syria, Northern Africa, and the middle east.

Banana Finger or crescent moon shaped fruit favored by monkeys and other mammals with discriminate tastes.

Bar Mitzvah An initiation ceremony usually marking the thirteenth birthday of a Jewish boy and signifying the beginning of religious responsibility.

Ben Yehuda Street Closed off street in Jerusalem where much shopping can be done in an open air mall fashion.

Biblical Harp Stringed instrument designed based on information found in the Bible, Talmud, and archeology.

Caesar's Barge A large flat bottomed boat presumably used by Roman Emperor Caesar who may have also had a flat bottom.

Camel A long necked desert mammal popular with the caravan set. Known for its humpage.

Canadian Don't get me started.

Chasids Religious Jews opposed to ritual laxity.

Dead Sea Body of salt water acting as border between Jordan and Israel which is also the lowest point on Earth and which is disappearing at a rate of thirty six inches per year which would have it completely gone within five hundred years of the publication of this book unless they get creative with canals from elsewhere.

Don Ho Native Hawaiian lounge singer known for being involved with tiny bubbles, hula dancers and the occasional Hookie Lau.

Epilady Machine famous for ripping hair out of ladies' legs.

fiesta Spanish for Hookie Lau. (See Don Ho)

Galilee Region in the north of Israel divided into upper and lower sections. Home of the Sea of Galilee, Israel's main fresh water source.

glossary A list of words and their definitions.

Golan Heights Hilly region in the north of Israel captured from Syria in 1967.

gravity That which causes things to fall.

Hagoshrim Kibbutz in the north of Israel where the Epilady was invented and home to at least three women named Michal.

Herod King of Jerusalem during the turn of the zero millennium famous for building lots of ancient things (though they were new at the time) including Masada and other things which are being dug up.

Hula Valley Valley in the north of Israel overlooked by the Golan Heights. Used to be swampy. Not so easy to ride a mountain bike through.

Israel A country in the middle east famous for it's high concentrations of Jews. Mentioned a lot in the Bible.

Jaffa Ancient port city in Israel outside of which Tel Aviv was built.

Jerusalem Ancient and modern capital of Israel.

kibbutz Communal living establishment where everyone shares everything.

Kotel Hebrew referring to the Western Wall.

luau A Hawaiian feast. (No Hawaiians are actually consumed.)

Mahane Yehuda Hebrew for Jewish Market. The open air Jewish Market in Jerusalem.

Marcella USC graduate student who takes a hell of a picture.

Masada Mountain top two-palaced fortress across the street from the Dead Sea built by King Herod probably to escape the cats in Jerusalem. Inhabited by Jewish Zealots who fended off the Romans for two years and then committed suicide rather than become slaves.

Michal Pronounced mee-<u>h</u>all. One of at least six different women in Israel.

Negev Desert Southern area of Israel known for it's hotness.

North Carolina One of the fifty states which make up the United States of America. Occasional travel destination for a particular Arab family.

Old City The ancient walled city of Jerusalem surrounded by the modern city.

Palestinians Arabs who co-occupy the land of Israel with Jews.

Play-Dough Pliable substance used for shaping and molding but not for baking. Non-toxic. Can be eaten if necessary.

Princess Leia Star Wars royal woman leader of the rebellion against the Empire. Originally with cinnamon rolls for hair.

Prozac An anti-depressant drug used to temper the behavior of far too many children who might be better served by the judicious implementation of Biblical Harps.

sabra Native born Israeli.

Shabbat Hebrew for Sabbath. Day of rest.

sheqels Main unit of currency in Israel.

Shikola Affectionate name for Joshua, the harmonica playing bus driver.

Syrian bunkers Places scattered throughout the Golan Heights where Syrian soldiers used to look out over places such as the Hula Valley and shoot at people.

Tamagotchi Electronic pets. Batteries included.

tarmac Material for surfacing roads, especially roads that airplanes travel on.

Tel Aviv Large modern coastal Israeli City. Sometimes referred to as the *New York* of Israel. Apples moderately sized.

Uzi Type of submachine gun designed and manufactured in Israel.

Western Wall The holiest spot for Jews. Last remaining wall of Herod's Temple. (even though other walls have since been excavated but just how thin do we need to spread our holy focus?)

Yad Vashem The Holocaust memorial and museum in Jerusalem.

yarmulke One of those things that Jews (traditionally men) wear on their heads.

Zionism Belief that there should be a Jewish homeland.

The author pictured with his head sticking out of an ancient hole.

Rick Lupert has been involved in the Los Angeles poetry community since 1990. He served for two years as a co-director of the Valley Contemporary Poets, a twenty-three year old non-profit organization which produces a regular reading series and publications out of the San Fernando Valley. His poetry has appeared in numerous magazines and literary journals, including *The Los Angeles Times, Chiron Review, Zuzu's Petals, Caffeine Magazine, Blue Satellite* and others. He recently edited *A Poet's Haggadah: Passover through the Eyes of Poets* anthology and is the author of ten other books: *Paris: It's The Cheese, I Am My Own Orange County, Mowing Fargo, I'm a Jew. Are You?, Stolen Mummies, I'd Like to Bake Your Goods, A Man With No Teeth Serves Us Breakfast* (Ain't Got No Press), *Lizard King of the Laundromat, Brendan Constantine is My Kind of Town* (Inevitable Press) and *Up Liberty's Skirt* (Cassowary Press). He has hosted the long running Cobalt Café reading series in Canoga Park since 1994 and is regularly featured at venues throughout Southern California.

Rick created and maintains the Poetry Super Highway, a major internet resource for poets. (PoetrySuperHighway.com)

Currently Rick works as the music teacher and graphic and web designer for Temple Ahavat Shalom in Northridge, CA and for anyone who would like to help pay his mortgage.

RICK'S OTHER BOOKS

A Man With No Teeth Serves Us Breakfast
Ain't Got No Press
May, 2007

I'd Like to Bake Your Goods
Ain't Got No Press
January, 2006

STOLEN MUMMIES
Ain't Got No Press
February, 2003

BRENDAN CONSTANTINE IS MY KIND OF TOWN
Inevitable Press
September, 2001

up liberty's skirt
Cassowary Press
March, 2001

I'm a Jew, Are You?
Cassowary Press
May, 2000

MOWING FARGO
Sacred Beverage Press
December, 1998

Lizard King of the Laundromat
The Inevitable Press
February, 1998

I Am My Own Orange County
Ain't Got No Press
May, 1997

Paris: It's The Cheese
Ain't Got No Press
May, 1996

For more information:
http://PoetrySuperHighway.com/